D-UNIT TALES

MILAN DJURASOVIC

D-UNIT TALES

Copyright @ 2023 by Milan Djurasovic.
All rights reserved.

Contact: DUnitTales@gmail.com

Written by Milan Djurasovic.
Cover Art by Milan Djurasovic.
Cover Design by Aleksandra Djurasovic.

Published by IngramSpark.
First Edition.
ISBN: 979-8-218-29962-0

TABLE OF CONTENTS

To my son, Nikolai.

D-UNIT TALES

Hunger

On the corner of D and 15th, like the gorgeous black marlin I am, I pounced on, snatched a shredded soft chicken taco out of a chubby kid's hand, and inhaled it before anyone could do anything about it. The kid started crying like the pampered little baby I'd suspected he was, and the owner of the taqueria, usually a sweet and accommodating fellow who sometimes gave me leftovers, carefully selected a bottle of the cheapest beer and threatened to throw it at my head. I stuck my tongue out and danced before him on one leg, daring him to do it.

He threw it, I caught it, had a drink, and laughed at him, but then the kid's dad blindsided me, poured his sticky soda on my head, and kneed me in the back. Anger and spite boiled in my chest, and a lively debate ensued when I could no longer disguise my outrage.

In language I am neither particularly ashamed nor proud of, I told the sneaky snake dad that he owed me a new shirt, to which he replied that I could go fuck myself because I owed his kid a chicken taco and an apology. His argument was sound, and his logic airtight. I am honest and admit that he easily won the initial round. But I am also the kind of man who will defend his honor at any cost to his dignity, and for my closing argument, I decided to undress and prance--like a beautiful wild cat-- around my foes in contracting circles. They shielded their eyes and were rendered speechless. Debate over! Checkmate! Swinging sack fires back! The same thing happens every time--you show a little skin in public, and these prudes, like roaches, scamper back to their caves.

When people are intellectually outmaneuvered, they often become consumed with rage, and if their mental age is that of an average adult pigeon and their egos fragile, sometimes they call the cops to fight their battles. The blue automatons found me fairly quickly, mostly because I didn't care to hide, and chased me around the block as I shouted a prayer and threw rocks and branches at them. They eventually subdued me and asked me to lower my tone.

I replied that I enjoyed voicing my opinions, that yelling is the optimal way to express specific emotions, and that they should try it because they were missing out. You would think that men of such a profession would care about the moral and bodily integrity of the people they are supposed to serve, but boy, would you be wrong. They treated me the way nobility used to treat their unruly serfs back in the days of Tsar Nicholas Pavlovich of Russia.

One of the blue men, weak in the body but rabid in the head, tripped me and punched my left kidney with his tiny fist. I christened him "Pork Chunk" and made fun of his small hands. He had to have the last word, so he punched my right kidney with all he had, which wasn't much and hurt only a little. I again called him by his new name, the proper name, figuring there were no kidneys left to hit.

But then others jumped in, and together, they flogged me for ten minutes straight. My mouth remained wide open, shouting all kinds of truths that came to mind. They finally bought my cooperation and silence with a can of warm soda and a stale peanut butter cookie. Even though my initial bid was another soft chicken taco, I thought it was just a transaction.

They searched all of my cavities at the hospital for hidden goodies, turned a hose over me, and gave me a scandalous gown to wear. I protested, demanded a cotton bathrobe and a cup of coffee with cream, and half-heartedly smacked a manservant for gawking and sneering at my demands. They panicked, and the autocrat in white hid behind the guards and ordered "booty juice" and solitary confinement. The sugary sap muddled my reason and weakened my knees. I sat on the floor, adjusted my underwear, and closed my eyes. I dreamed about Grandma's cornbread.

A youthful virgin woke me up in the morning. She ignored my grogginess and asked about my coping skills and leisure interests. I told her about the pectoral cross with which I was decorated for my service to mankind. She wrote on her pad that my replies were tangential and had no earthly motives. I was still drained but restless and anxious. I begged her to ask the autocrat in white for more "booty juice." She told me a second dose was a long shot for the uninsured. As a compromise, I was promised coffee and crackers in exchange for attending group therapy and taking part in a tournament of Scattergories.

Lack of insurance, my compliance with the protocol, and an easy victory in the tournament earned me discharge documents. The autocrat placed the certificate of completion in my hands, along with words of encouragement and detailed directives on how to live my life. Most of his ideas made little sense, but few were sensible and valuable—I should wash my ass more often.

As the titan manservants escorted me through the cafeteria towards the exit, the kitchen stewards rolled their carts on which there were dozens of glorious soft-shelled tacos. With a submissive demeanor and moisture on my lips, I looked at the pudgier guard, thinking he would understand. But he shook his melon firmly and gestured for me to get the fuck out.

Never About Me

We had an unlikely love triangle, but each of us benefited from it while it lasted, and I was confident that our intentions were genuine.

Brad was a Vietnam War veteran, not much of a speaker, but was good with numbers and knew all there was to know about acute, obtuse, and right angles. Pythagorean theorem he knew like the back of his hand. Brad was in his early seventies then but had an upright posture, two strong legs with thighs as big as two sacks of flour, bulging veins all over his arms, and a chiseled chin you could cut Parmesan cheese on. I told him he could advertise cigarettes or cowboy boots for a living, but he said he was not interested in fame and only took from life that which was in perfect harmony with his unassuming nature. He wanted to grow tomatoes and hunt deer, and he invited us to live with him in his cabin upon our discharge from the hospital.

Donna was two decades younger—a distinguished actress, passionate about justice and beauty. She was to be our Cleopatra, a sacred flower of our future household. We would provide her with water and sunshine, and she would inspire us with her wisdom and untarnished ideals. At the time, I was two years younger than Brad, and my talent was my wit, which was crude due to old age, but it was still quick and helpful in interactions with doctors and nurses. Taking care of household chores was the price I had agreed to pay to evade the long and nasty claws of solitude, which, before meeting the two of them, was how I thought I was destined to spend the rest of my life.

Even in its earliest stages, our partnership was not without problems. The sexual tension between Brad and Donna made me feel inadequate and ostracized at times, even though I had ceased competing for affection ever since, during my first hospitalization, a piece of copper wire was forcefully inserted in my testicles to blunt all of my senses. But, unlike Brad, whose stories were boring and always without an aim, I could stimulate Donna intellectually. She would come to me with her thoughts and anxieties and to Brad for cuddles. Brad respected my intellect; I tolerated his dimness, which is how we learned to get along.

We went to all therapy sessions together and took the medication we were prescribed in the hope that we would be discharged as early as possible so that we could embark on our adventure. During therapy, I marveled at Donna's confidence and wisdom. We learned more about human urges from her than from our doctors and group leaders. Because she had been trained as a professional actress, Donna could laugh and cry on cue, feign indignance and compassion, and convince anyone of anything in seconds. During one of her daily pranks, she fooled me into thinking that preserving self-respect is a stronger motivator than sex. It sounds funny now, but Donna genuinely had me fooled. She allowed me to humiliate myself for an entire week by defending her assertion in discussions with nurses and staff in our unit. She was the most outstanding actress alive, our precious jewel, and our duty was to help everyone around notice her shine.

But Brad, the old goat that he was, completely neglected and aborted our mission the moment the voluptuous vixen arrived on the unit. During what was to be our last group at the facility, the shapely maneater sat next to Brad for her first meeting, regarded him with sympathetic curiosity, and rewarded his every movement and word with a sugary smile. She felt his knotty biceps, complimented hardened blisters on his long fingers, and helped him complete our daily progress questionnaire. He drew her hand towards his lips, bowed like a gentleman, and kissed her knuckles three times.

The group leader tried to separate them, and the girl threw a fit. She rolled up her shirt, pulled out one of her breasts, and then started wiping her erect nipple with a wet tissue. Upon seeing the breast, the group leader and Brad became rattled for vastly different reasons. The group leader was afraid for his job. He looked around to see if any of the unit nurses or staff had witnessed the incident before he told the girl to leave the room. On the other hand, Brad was just a horny old goat, and he reacted the way horny old goats do when they see an erect nipple.

Brad jumped to her defense and called the group leader a "silly charlatan" who never taught us anything and could only regurgitate someone else's meaningless statements as though they were his own. He then turned towards the new girl, calling her a "celestial creature" and, after a brief stutter, "an amazing actress bound for greatness."

All this commotion took place right in front of poor Donna. I caught her looking down at her torso and legs, pinching the fat on her belly, and observing the fold with her sad eyes. She then crumpled her group questionnaire and threw it at Brad's forehead. She missed and hit his gaping mouth instead. The paper flew in, hit the back of his throat, and made him cough.

Brad stood up, pointed at Donna, and told her that she was a spiteful old hag, that he never truly loved her, and that he saw her as nothing more than a short-term distraction to help ease the boredom and frustration in this hellhole of a hospital. He said that he had no use for a "washed-up actress," that "girlish love" is what he is after, and that the smell of youthful skin makes him feel alive. Brad then crumpled his group questionnaire and threw it at Donna's nose, but he missed badly and hit another patient's ear. The patient who got smacked was not the one to mess around with, and he instantly threw himself at Brad and started pummeling his square chin with heavy elbows.

A code was called by the head nurse, and burly male staff from other units rushed in and started tackling us. Donna and I were pinned in the same corner of the common room.

"Let's talk about it later and see if we can salvage any of this," I pleaded. "I know we can. We don't need Brad." I wept aloud so that she could not ignore me.

"This was never about you," is all she said.

I was then carried away by the floor staff, given emergency medication, and in the stillness of my room, Donna's hurtful words rang softly and lulled me to sleep.

Apology

Some knuckle-nuts be power trippin' for no reason. I don't get it, man. They be doin' it just because they can: immitatin' big ballers, pretendin' to be a CEO or some shit like that. But they fools though; they know they ain't got shit to they name, just slavin' for a true boss who be tellin' 'em to bully us like we li'l kids. Mofos heads be as big as watermelons and nuts no bigger than two Peanut M&M's. Gotta be yolked and willin' to fuck a senior citizen in management to eke out a livin' doin' what they do: chest bumpin' each other as they patrol the unit in extra small company polos, shushin' us cuckoos when we get loud, and clampin's down on our God-given rights. Let me educate you on what I mean.

We was watchin' basketball in the day room. While we debatin' who the GOAT is, and this young fella was sayin' Lebron this and Lebron that, he big, he strong, he don't get hurt, he a freight train, he the best passer in the history of the game, his IQ outta this world, 20/20 vision, turns scrubs into heroes. I just sat back in my chair and kept repeatin', "Six fo' six and the one you be talkin' about--four fo' ten in the finals." I said, "MJ psycho, man, a requisite for any GOAT in any walk of life. Psychos at the top of businesses, psychos rule Hollywood, psychos doin' psycho shit in Congress, psychos run this hospital. You can't compete with psychos— they think they on a mission from God. They be shootin' bazookas while the rest be clawin' and stabbin' through life with toothpicks. They wired differently, little bro."

"Lebron won with three different teams and would kill MJ in the post if they matched up," a different young fool tried to get in on it.

"Lebron soft!" I said. "He don't have no post game. He too stiff and clumsy. Zero fluidity to his game—can't do a spin move without takin' nine steps. He want none of that turn-around fadeaway smoke. His armor full of chinks. MJ hard in the clutch!" I said. "He nut five times and remain stiff as he wreck they heads and take they souls fo' keepsake. Lebron limp in the clutch! The only thing hard about Lebron is bricks he be throwing at the rim when he need to hit a shot at the end of games. Let me just say this: the odds of Lebron hittin' two free throws in a row … in the clutch … is about as good as you takin' home that pretty little nurse over there."

We was havin' a good time clownin', but then this big boy, this buzzkilla', decided to pop his big-ass melon in to tell us to stop yellin and settle down or we gon' have quiet time for two hours. The asshole made me angry as hell. I hate bullyin-ass bitches. We ain't got shit to do on the unit but talk, and he decided we can't even do that because big boy's ears sensitive and can't handle a little noise.

"Who the fuck is you?" I said. "Is you the FBI? Is you maybe ICE tryin' to catch a Mexican? We all citizens here, and we already caged, so just move on with yo' day and leave us alone, man."

The company lapdog got his lazy-ass off the chair and started frontin' like I did somethin' to him. His pride was smashed--can't let any pretty nurses see him get punked by a loony scrub.

"I'll tell you who the fuck I am," he said. "I am the guy who runs around gettin' you fresh towels, clean gowns, and socks, bringin' you your food and juice, buyin' snacks for all y'all with my own money instead of spendin' it on my kids. I've treated all y'all with respect, and you gon' show me up 'cause I told you to be quiet for a second? Nah, dawg. That's not how it's gon' go down."

I turned to the young gun I'd been debatin' and said: "Yo, five bucks I knock his giant bitch-ass out with one punch?"

Big boy got Dead Sea salty, fumin' like an Icelandic volcano. He got all up in my grill, demandin' silence and apologies. He was breathin' down my neck, spittin' on my face as he yelled and clapped his hands like he 'bout to do somethin'.

I stepped back, wiped the spit off my face, and said: "You dumb mothafucka… How can I apologize and be silent at the same time? That shit make no sense. Explain to me how I can do both… And why you standing so close, bruh? At least give me an umbrella or somethin'. Shit… Comin' in here preaching about the rules and respect with his stank ass breath. Go on and get you some gum and leave us be. We ain't doin' shit to anyone."

He started flexin' on me, poundin' his chest, wavin' his thick sausage fingers in my face. He threaten' meds if I don't chill the fuck out. He said how two days ago he got me a soda and gave me his own t-shirt, how I need to reciprocate and show him the same level of respect, and while he was talkin', I was thinkin' to myself: "Duh, you clown-ass ignoramus; ain't that your fuckin' job?" But I ain't no fool. If I have to take a bullet, it best be for somethin' that gon' last. I wasn't about to shoot myself in the foot to prove a point to a dummy who ain't gon' get it anyway.

I clasped my hands behind my back, and spoke soft: "We was conversin', discussin' sports and havin' a good time. Us poor folk, who suffer from chronic brokeassness—all we have is chatter. What else we gon' discuss-- what wine go with what fish? French documentaries? Leave these people alone, man. Let them have they say, be experts in somethin' fo' a minute. A lil' noise never hurt nobody."

For a minute I thought I got to the Guv'nor, but the fuck I did. He snatched the remote, turned off the TV, and walked out. The young man stood up and was about to say somethin', but I motioned to him to stay put.

"You've gotta be slick about it. You gotta get 'em when they don't see it comin', when the battlefield ain't so uneven. But don't even trip, little bro… When I catch that donkey on the street, I am goin' MJ on his punk ass, put a dent in his ego, and get us our apology."

Good Intentions

I explained in detail the events that brought me to my present state of mind. Still, the doctor seemed to be in disbelief that such a "trifle" could make a man climb a tree and throw himself on the windshield of a moving vehicle.

I then explained that my intention was to land on the sidewalk but that I had underestimated my athletic ability and that if I had heard the approaching vehicle, I would have waited for it to pass by before jumping. Besides, my head barely nicked the windshield, and the driver reported no significant damage to the car. I even helped clean the blood that smeared the car's hood as we waited for the paramedics.

While the doctor kept probing and asking all kinds of irrelevant questions about drugs I was on at the time of the incident, my family's history of depression and psychosis, the importance of healthy routines and taking my medication regularly, I kept shifting the conversation to the realization that I no longer could bear pretending to be the person people wanted me to be—a sensible human being. So, I cut him off and spoke directly from my soul.

"You can prescribe whatever medication you want," I told him. "You can keep me here as long as you think is necessary, but I would really like for you to sit with me and listen until I finish telling you about the 'trifle.'" The doctor was visibly annoyed but agreed reluctantly.

"She was going through a prolonged period of heat, and I thought it'd be best to take advantage of it instead of leaving it to fate," I explained to the doctor. "Over our first two months together, I was able to convince her, and myself to an extent, that I was the type women could fall in love with and not regret it. I became really good at manipulating my thoughts, and for a while, I felt like any other happy fool—willfully ignorant and arrogant. During those months, many of my chronic doubts and fears vanished. I even stopped thinking about what I could have been had I not allowed the weight of other people's opinions to crush my self-esteem, my plans, and how different my life would have turned out if I had been a little bolder and more ambitious."

The doctor shifted in his chair and raised his eyebrows after each sentence. He had other patients to assess, and the growling in his stomach told me that he had not yet had his lunch. We had been talking for about ten minutes, and only a few items on his assessment sheet had been checked off. I asked him politely to stop squeaking and that I would answer all of his questions as soon as I was finished talking about what was on my mind.

"I convinced myself that she had tapped into a part of my nature which, up until then, I wasn't aware of. That was the first time in my adulthood and the only time I thought I had a chance to be like everyone else: good to myself and deaf and dumb to my surroundings. I could devote everything I had to her now that I was free of any other obligations and no longer consumed with vain aspirations. I told her I was fond of smooth jazz and a staunch vegan. I also lied that I loved cats and regularly signed petitions about preserving this body of water and protecting that endangered rodent. But I lied only because I really wanted her to like me.

"She often regurgitated sweet little phrases about how I had restored her faith in men and what a breath of fresh air my outlook on life was. I learned to tolerate that kind of silly talk and allowed myself to get carried away. What mattered to me was that she was raw and vulnerable even when she used clichés to express how she felt, and that vulnerability gave me confidence and made me feel needed. It also made me think that I was in charge, a manly man—big dick energy radiated from every pore during those days. My lady was a neurotic mess with a tendency to overanalyze her every social interaction and blame herself for every conflict she was a part of. Most men would scoff at such a person, but I find that kind of stuff endearing."

I don't know if he was trying to be sarcastic, but at this point, the doctor asked me how I could let go of such a rare connection. He wanted to know why the bond I shared with my lady friend wasn't a good enough reason to remain hopeful that the relationship could be repaired or that another could be formed with someone else.

To avoid beating around the bush, I told him that I could not bear seeing a woman weep on my account, that it filled me with angst I didn't know what to do with. I told him this: "She started dieting and exercising for me, and I am just not equipped to deal with that kind of pressure and responsibility. She lost a lot of weight and had to buy a new wardrobe. Here, I had an innocent creature running in place, spending money, lifting things, sweating, getting all red in the face to be more attractive to me—a fraud who has never been able to properly do or appreciate anything in life. I couldn't watch her humiliate herself like that. I decided to break things off and take the blame, thinking that would help preserve her dignity."

The doctor listened attentively and even thanked me for sharing my story. I thanked him for his time and then fulfilled my promise by helping him check off the boxes on his assessment sheet. We then agreed on the length of my stay and what kind of new anxiety medication I could try taking. We shook hands, and I felt embarrassed for being rude to him initially.

Before leaving, he told me I should give myself some credit for acting on good intentions and that most people would have kept the charade going until it imploded on its own. Honestly, the doctor's parting remark inspired no confidence in me and only made me feel awkward, but it was a kind gesture, and I repaid it with a limp wave and a forced smile.

Realness

I do it for free food and the bed. I admit myself to the hospital and tell the receptionist I need to be placed in unit D because the voices in my head are getting louder and telling me to jump in front of a moving vehicle. I do all this monthly to eat and sleep regularly for a few days to build up enough energy for another try at "success" on the outside. I am not joking when I say that the bed and the food are the primary motivation, but another reason is the need to be around real people. That's all you get on unit D—real, honest people. I wouldn't cry a single tear if the outside world disappeared off the face of the earth, but don't dare touch or try to change unit D, or we will have major problems.

The world has changed a lot since I was a little kid. It lost its realness sometime in the early eighties. You can still find bits of it on Richards Boulevard in the tent camp among the OGs, but there isn't any shade there, and you risk getting your cans and smokes stolen. That is about the only place in the city where I can be true to who I am on the inside. No one believes in anything everywhere else; they just pretend to live by the old code. They can talk your ear off, but they are just fantasizing and imitating what they hear on the radio, and it's all fake.

Back in the day, people's thoughts and actions were solid as a rock. Life wasn't any easier back then—for me, at least--but it was simple and true. People knew the value of what they had and where they would deposit it. There were fewer paths, but you picked one and rolled with it until the end. There was no wavering like there is today. You played the cards you were dealt like a man.

People are blind nowadays, and their thoughts are wobbly. One moment, they argue over this one thing, and then they moan about the opposite with a different person. And that's somehow cool with everyone. If today I say that I like yellow the most and then have doubts about it later in the evening, I can still sleep tight knowing that red could be my favorite color tomorrow morning and no one will ever call me out on it. And people really seem to be okay living this way. Gone are the days when a person was a proud slave to their principles. Loyal customers and dedicated dreamers willing to catch a bullet for their truth are nearly all gone.

Don't get me wrong, there are plenty of posers in unit D as well. Wesley "The Weasel" Jackson is one of those shifty dudes that comes to mind. He is a go-along-motherfucker, but he lies and snitches not because he is a dishonest little bitch, but because the dude's scared. When he smells a hairy alpha on the unit, he attaches himself and tags along to keep people he's indebted to from smacking him around. If the alpha is fond of his tongue, knowing that he is safe, he'll even get gutsy and flip people off when they remind him of his dues. But Wesley's kind is rare on the unit. It's mostly straight shooters who come there—people who know what the game is about. Let me tell a quick story to paint a clearer picture for you.

A young man was on the unit a few months back, fresh and frail, just past the line separating boys from men. This skinny youngster would take the Bible with him even to the shitter, and he never missed a chance to praise the all-forgiving Lord. Every morning, he'd ask me if I had heard the good news, and whether or not my answer was yes, he'd tell me to get my shit together because his buddy Jesus was coming for my soul. After the sermon, I'd ask him how his morning was going, and he'd always reply with: "I feel the same way I felt yesterday and the same way I'll feel tomorrow—blessed!"

One day, a thick-set lady of very explosive demeanor was brought to the unit, and the young buck, without offering a greeting or introducing his skinny ass, asked her if she had heard the good news. (I have to make known here that I'd been the lady's customer on a few occasions in the distant past, so I knew she did not like to be spoken to unless dollars or dope were your opening lines). She walked up calmly to the young preacher, and as soon as he was within arm's reach, she smacked him around like a piñata until she was restrained by the staff. The young man sat quietly in his chair and took the beating without moving a finger. He wanted to prove that he practiced what he preached and was ready to turn the other cheek a million times if necessary.

As she kicked and fought the staff on the ground, the scrawny boy, spitting out bloody saliva with each word, begged them to be gentle and to forgive the lady because that was what his buddy Jesus wanted. "She doesn't know any better!" he kept crying out as they turned her into a starfish, pinning her limbs to the floor.

The young fellow offered peace the following day by handing the girl his breakfast. She took the plate without saying a word, stood up, and threw the hot oatmeal in his face. The glazed mush slid down his cheeks, and it must have hurt bad, but he didn't dare wipe it off.

"Defend yourself, you pussy!" she said. "Do something about it, or I'll punch your teeth out."

"Even if they sin against you a hundred times and never repent, you must forgive them," the boy closed his eyes and whispered to himself.

The lady then stood up and slapped the boy at least five times, yelling, "I repent!" each time her hand landed on his bony cheeks. "Grow a pair and hit me back!" she kept yelling at him. But the boy sat motionless. He was as relaxed as a cup of green tea, and ready for more.

Tired and defeated, she sat back down, finished eating her breakfast, and after the last sip of coffee, said, "You don't wanna be Jesus, boy. Jesus was a quitter, was bullied because he just let shit happen to him."

Now if this little back-and-forth between these two individuals isn't the definition of real, then I don't fucking know what real is. They duked it out like that every day for a week and, as an impartial observer, I'd say it was a clear draw. I do not know whose truth won, but that doesn't matter here. All I am saying is that if you can prove me wrong and show me just one example of this kind of realness anywhere on the outside, I'll admit my mistake and repent as many times as necessary.

The Price is Right

He was nicer than all the other doctors and group therapists they threw at us for treatment and entertainment. I'd even say that he cared for us. He brought us all kinds of knickknacks from the dollar store he'd buy with his money, mainly arts and crafts supplies, holiday decorations, board games, and snacks. Yes, all of it was cheap, and he obviously didn't spend a fortune, but credit where credit is due; he was the only one who did it.

We could tell other group leaders' hearts were not in it like his. They were there for a paycheck and nothing more, always half-assing it, day after day, repeating the same topics about how we need to be better and kinder to ourselves--as if I'd be any happier if my toenails were cleaner and my hair combed. "Tell me three positive things about you," they'd say. "How about two short-term goals?"

They would give us coloring pages when they ran out of stupid questions. We'd color like maniacs because there was nothing else to do on the unit.

The guy didn't have to, but he explained that their supervisors make them cover topics with "measurable goals" and that these silly questions about our positive qualities and plans for the future are asked to help them cover their asses when auditors come around. That made sense because they never did anything about our real concerns and emotions; all they did was number them.

The guy covered those boring topics, too, but he'd also talk about other stuff. He'd also let us chat about anything we wanted, as long as we didn't cuss or insult someone in the room. He'd say that any conversation is therapeutic as long as all sides are willing participants with good intentions.

I am not smart, but I felt like it when he'd listen to me ramble about my obsessions. He made me feel as if I was revealing some unseen wisdom and always treated me as his equal.

One day, he came to the group and gathered everyone not sleeping into the common room. He left the door open so other doctors and nurses could hear him.

"After you get discharged, don't come here no more," he said. "This place can't help you. You'll just get sicker while you're in here."

"Fuck this place!" I said in agreement. "Are we still having a group meeting, though? If not, I was gonna ask if you maybe came through on those shoes you promised."

"Not today," he said. "I just stopped by to tell you guys to never come back to this so-called hospital after you leave. Avoid this place like the plague that it is."

"I am tired of eating carbs and watching '50 First Dates' all day every day," said the young girl who hadn't talked at all since she arrived on the unit some week or so ago.

"Doctor comes in," said Jerry, a good bud of mine, "fist bumps air instead of my knuckles as if I am some kind of leper, and says, 'thank you very much, Jerry, for being calm and for fist bumping some air. This little pleasantry is an important part of your treatment and will cost you fifty thousand dollars.' Then he comes the next morning and says, 'Hi, Jerry, are you hearing any voices today? No, okay, great. Zero auditory hallucinations amount to another five hundred thousand dollars, Jerry, but since you are one of our regulars, we'll knock it down five percent.' He then says, ' Do you want to harm yourself or others?' At that point, I just shake my big ol' head instead of answering because each word out of my mouth is another grand out of my pocket."

"Jerry is right," said the guy. "It's all about the money; they don't care about you. That's why I am out of here. I am tired of feeling guilty for partaking; I want to be able to sleep at night."

"You get on out of here, teacher," said Jerry. Jerry stood up and shook the guy's hand. "They don't deserve you. My ass is outta here on Monday, and I ain't never coming back! I like it better at the other hospital across town; they give you smoke breaks and sloppy joes on Tuesdays."

The guy fixed the collar on his jacket, wished everyone luck, thanked us for listening, and walked out of the unit a proud man. We applauded each of his steps, and just before he disappeared behind the unit doors, he victoriously raised his fist in the air.

"A fuckin' hero!" said Jerry. "Look at his fine ass go!"

I wish this was all I had to say, but a fucking hero the guy pretended to be for only about a minute. He was no different than any other con he worked with. He actually was worse because he knew better. He threw his little tantrum and took a few hours to think about his options, but that was the end of his revolt. I can't claim to know what they told him or gave him to shut him up, but the guy came back the following day to talk to us about coping skills.

"What the fuck is this shit?" said Jerry as soon as he saw him enter the unit the following morning.

"Hey, backstabber, what happened?" I said as I walked up to him.

The guy knew my name but called me "Sir" and told me to back up.

I said, "I'll back up when you give me those shoes you owe me."

"They are in my car," he said. "I'll run and grab them, and you get ready for the group. Deal?"

And he came through. They fit almost perfectly and still had that new shoe smell. After putting them on, I lost the right to continue bitching. But, since Jerry didn't get shoes, he didn't have to hold punches. And he didn't. Jerry was on his ass until the staff removed him from the group.

A Nobody

He woke me up when he sat on the edge of my bed and leaned over to whisper something long and dry in my ear. I was groggy, disoriented, and a little angry, and for a moment, I thought I was back home.

"Is that you, Derek?" I spoke.

"It's not Derek," he said, "but maybe I could be your Derek if I tried hard enough. Although I doubt it… I don't know. Maybe I have what it takes to be your Derek."

I sat up and picked at the corners of my eyes to remove the hardened snot that covered them. Once my sight wasn't as hazy, I saw that sitting next to me was a young-looking man with curved noodles for eyebrows, two large buttons for eyes, and a meaty dumpling for a nose.

"And who are you to me?" I said.

"I am a nobody who badly wants to be accepted as somebody," he said. "But for now, I can try to be Derek. But only if that's what you want."

"But why are you here?" I spoke. I was a bit scared but mainly angry, and the cracks in my voice probably gave me away.

"It's a long story," he said, "but I'll try to make it brief. I ate something wonderful, a medicinal herb I stole from a shop. A few minutes after eating it, the Devil appeared above my head. Devils, to be exact… I saw four of them, but I told the nurse there was only one. They extend your hold if you tell them you see or hear too many things. One Devil they can tolerate, but if you see two or more, they'll say, 'This guy is not right in the head and needs our help.' Then they use a permanent marker to write it all down in their big blue book."

"What I meant to say is… what are you doing sitting on my bed?" I spoke. He apologized for not asking permission and then explained that my face pleased him and that my odor, especially my energy, was to his taste.

"I was trying to use your positive vibes as a shield from the Devils," he said. "They are scared of everything wonderful and glossy. Four Devils with four horns each have been after me for something I did long ago. Number four means death in Japanese, and I keep avoiding them because I don't want to die before I learn how to live."

"I really don't know what you mean," I said. "Obviously, you are a somebody. Everybody is a somebody."

"Except me!" he said. "I never had parents, no brothers, no sisters, no relatives, no dogs or cats. I have no space of my own. I've never decorated anything in my life. I've never told a joke. I never had a wallet; even if I did, it'd be empty. Not too long ago, I came close to knowing a man I thought could be my friend, but he quickly realized that I was a nobody, and that was the end."

"What did you do to make him leave?" I spoke. "Did you sit on his bed while he was sleeping?"

"He met somebody, and that somebody lured him away from me," he said.

"When I met my friend, if you can call him that, he had a lot of trouble on his hands. He was sitting on a park bench, spitting out pumpkin seeds, his feet bare and filthy, and he was terrified he had the virus. I sat next to him, offered him a tissue, and we were on good terms five minutes later. His vibes were similar to yours—sparkly and upbeat. We saw each other every morning for almost a month and had a good thing going--I traded my meals and loose change for his energy. One evening, he asked me to go down by the river to talk about something that had been on his mind for a few days."

"So… What happened?" I spoke.

"He said that a nobody has to connect with a somebody to have a chance in life. He said that two nobodies equal a negative and that a nobody paired with a somebody results in a neutral, which was the best people like us could hope for. I thought differently. When multiplied, I thought that two nobodies could cancel each other out and, in that way, become a positive, which is obviously better than neutrality. I wanted to express my disagreement, but I remained silent and only listened because a nobody's opinion doesn't amount to much. He spent the night with me and was no longer there when I woke. My shoes were also gone, but I would have given them to him anyway. I thought crying would be a good idea, but I was never taught how. Instead of crying, I bit my lip and made it bleed, and then I walked along the river for hours, spitting blood in the water, thinking how this is all there will ever be for me, up to the day I die."

Before I could tell the scrawny fellow that he was a somebody to me, a mental health technician barged into the room and shouted at him to get out. He stood up quickly, thanked me for sharing my energy, and was taken to a more acute unit shortly after as punishment for breaking the rules. I asked the staff to take my sweatshirt to him, but they said that sharing clothes was prohibited at the hospital.

A Prayer

My old roommate left early in the morning, and my new roommate arrived late at night. My old roommate left the hospital shouting at her doctor for allowing her rights to be abused during her stay, whereas the new one was unusually silent and compliant when they brought her in. Patients brought in late at night are typically under the influence of something, and they kick and scream until everyone on the unit is up and about.

My new roommate was not like that at all. She was extremely calm and obedient. She immediately took a shower, asked for clean socks and underwear, neatly folded her clothes, and politely asked for them to be washed. She thanked the staff for their help and tried to shake their hand, but they only gave her a fist bump—a strict policy at the hospital aimed to prevent the spread of germs, quarrels, and lawsuits.

She made herself comfortable on the bed and gazed at the ceiling for a while. The moonlight made patches of her long white hair glisten. She wheezed as she exhaled, and her almost inaudible sneezes came in pairs. She used her inhaler, and once she regained her breath and the sneezing subsided, she closed her eyes, crossed herself three times, and whispered the following prayer:

"Dear God, thank you for all you have done and continue to do for me. Thank you for the people in my life, for the learned lessons, for the little things I try my best to recognize and cherish, and for the countless blessings I have failed to notice or have already forgotten about. Please forgive my sins, big and small, accidental ones, and those I've done on purpose, those I am aware of, and those I have failed to see and accept. Dear Mary, Mother of God, thank you for all the blessings you've sent my way, and please forgive all of my failings, which are many and which have hurt a lot of people. Dear Saint Nicholas of Myra, the patron of my family, thank you for protecting us and for all the pleasant moments in life, which are many, and for which I have to be more thankful. Please forgive me for not recognizing and appreciating those moments as I should have. Forgive my selfishness and self-pity. Forgive me for taking the good things and good times for granted. I recognize that I am sinful and regret it even though my repeated sins may say otherwise."

She then opened her eyes and successfully subdued another sneezing fit by rubbing her eyes with the bottom of her shirt. She took a deep breath and crossed herself three more times before continuing the prayer.

"Thank you, archangels Michael and Gabriel… Thank you for the shelter and food I receive, and please forgive me for not being there for those who need me and for taking advantage of those who are kind to me. Forgive me for seeing their kindness as a weakness. Please guide and care for my little one and keep him safe until I recover and can take over. Please protect Dad and give him at least another five years of good health so we can talk and play cards many more times. Please protect my sister Joanne and send a kind-hearted gentleman friend her way so she doesn't grow old alone."

I wanted to wait for her to finish before scratching an itch on my shoulder, but I couldn't fight it any longer and went for it. I interrupted her when I turned to my side and reached for the spot. I dug into my skin with my nails, and it felt so good that I, a lifelong atheist, experienced an urge to thank God for small things in life. Ten minutes later, she finished her prayer when she was sure I was fast asleep.

"Dear St. John and St. George, thank you for all the joys in my life. Please forgive me for my self-centeredness and for forgetting about people much worse off than me. I also pray for them and wish everyone to have enough of everything for a good life. Please punish greed and smite those who keep more than they need to live comfortably. If you think that I am a hypocrite, that I belong to the dark side and am a part of the problem, don't hesitate to smite me as well, but please know that I am trying my best to bring the light of Your ways into this world."

That was the end of her prayer. She crossed herself three more times and was fast asleep less than five minutes later. She slept through the night with a gleeful little smirk on her face. I haven't witnessed such serenity since then.

Guilty Pleasures

I knew what I did could make him lose his job, and I did it anyway. We all have urges, but the difference between you and me is that most of you can tame yours. On the other hand, I just go for it without thinking and deal with the consequences later.

So, this skinny dame kept following me around the unit, complimenting my eyes. I tried to shed her off by telling her I had a girlfriend named Tina who had D-cup titties and a big ole butt, but she didn't want to hear it. Her mind was made up, and her pursuit of delight would not stop.

Now Jerome was a cool dude, probably my favorite staff at the hospital--big as hell but would only get physical if some asshole threw a punch at him first or started beating up on other patients. He strictly followed the rules, but he was never stingy about seconds during meals and even took some of us who didn't have red bands and weren't allowed to leave the unit for outdoor exercise and leisure.

Ten days into my stay, I was anxious and sexually motivated. On the outside, I have sex daily, and ten days without any action was sheer torture. I'd get random boners just eating breakfast or playing checkers with other dudes. I had a roommate who'd stay in bed all day, and, unlike him, I've never been able to beat off in another man's presence. Also, my thoughts get scrambled, and I get easily distracted when standing up, so jacking off in the shower wasn't an option. I need a comfortable sofa and privacy to give my meat a proper beating. So, imagine my frustration and consider that this skinny admirer was always around, and, on top of that, they put her in a single room. "Fuck it," I thought, "if she really wants it that bad, she can get it."

The floor staff do their rounds every fifteen minutes if they are willing to do their job as required. That means they walk up and down the hallway and scribble a brief note on each of us. "Johnny is feuding with the doorknob again," or "Jackie is pacing and whispering to self about the end of times." They spy on us like that all day, and I pick up a book every time I hear their footsteps and pretend to read, so all of my notes probably say: "T's at his desk again, geeking out, bettering himself."

Well, I found out that on Wednesdays, my homeboy Jerome works at his other job before his shift at the hospital. I figured he'd come in tired and forge his first set of rounds to sneak in a power nap. And that's precisely what happened. He came in, went over the rules, and told us what he expected from us, and he then dozed off in his chair.

So… I snuck into the girl's room and let her sandjob the nob with her parched lips. The poor thing worked on it for at least twenty minutes, but I couldn't nut because of all the medication I was on then. That is how Jerome and I got got by the system's stooges, and they fired the gentle giant on the spot. He was fuming, said that they never appreciated him anyway, and walked out with tears in his eyes. And I blame myself, but I also blame my asshole roommate for monopolizing the room. None of this would have happened if I had five minutes, twice a day, to myself. Stupid, selfish asshole. Both him but mostly me.

I tried standing up for Jerome and told my doctor what a good worker he was, how he helped so many of us, made us feel safe and comfortable, and encouraged us to use our coping skills to hash things out instead of fighting. But, as expected, the doctor dismissed my ramblings, upped my dosage of everything I was on, and prescribed some additional shit I didn't want to take.

So, Jerome got fucked over, and the new stuff they gave me made me feel dead inside. Except I still feel terrible whenever I think about what happened to Jerome, and I keep picturing his kids going to school in cheap sneakers. I made a promise that when I get discharged, I am going to find him so that he could beat the shit out of me, or at least tell him that the blowjob wasn't worth it and that now I have tiny blisters on my dick as a reminder of my transgression. I don't know if that would help Jerome, but it would surely help me get some sleep.

I broke things off with the skinny dame after the incident. She first wept and then said that I looked like a battered dog and that she didn't want my skinny dick anyway. She was obviously stuck in a place of hurt, and I wasn't about to retaliate and make things worse. Like many times before, I just walked away from the mess I caused.

But honestly, she should have known what she was getting into…
Unit D is where you might find a decent friend who can hook you up
with some good shit, but it's not where you look for a friend. Luckily, she
prevailed in her hearing this morning and is getting picked up by her
sister in the afternoon. I wish her all the best from the bottom of my heart.

A Hero Of Our Time

We started the morning group by reading a rather sad but hopeful fable about a man who helped deliver a moth by snipping bits of its cocoon to help it crawl out. The man's good-intentioned deed ended up depriving the moth of the necessary struggle, rendering its frame feeble, its wings withered, and its existence miserable.

The patients were then asked to relate instances of personal hardship and to determine whether or not those experiences made them stronger and more resilient. Two patients answered affirmatively. One gave me a choice to keep my clichés at home or shove them up Kelly Clarkson's ass, but nearly all of them had something to say on the topic, which is a rare occurrence during my groups.

Referring to the moth story, one patient said that regardless of one's intentions, knowing when and how to help a fellow human requires a lot of awareness and emotional intelligence. She said, "If you tell me to calm down when I'm blazin', your face is for surely getting smacked!" A different patient wasn't sure if her hardships made her resilient, but she was confident that they made her more compassionate and less judgmental of others who are "going through shit." She said: "You ain't ever finna hear someone who's been on the streets tell a woman she reeks of BO and piss cuz you been there yourself." Another patient said that some struggles in life could be valuable but that dealing with "so much crap day after day" has made him bitter and paranoid of motherfuckers who want for free everything he's worked very hard for.

When I asked them about specific issues they could overcome, my patients were just as receptive and sociable. One gentleman said he no longer spends money on "wild women" because his past mistakes had taught him that "all of them are backstabbers" who take advantage of honest men. One of the ladies remarked that telling her friends to "disappear" was the best thing she could have done to regain the self-respect and confidence needed to pursue a more dynamic lifestyle. Josh, who usually never speaks during groups, raised his hand next and shared the following insightful observation.

He said: "I believe in God and read the Bible every day, but, honestly, some parts in it are confusing as fuck. Someone needs to rewrite it without all the numbers and parables. Just delete all the mumbo-jumbo and tell us how to live instead of us guessing. I still haven't figured out whose face is supposed to get slapped and how many times. When I was in jail, if you turned the other cheek, your ass got raped twice before you could get a word in. Abraham fooled around with Sara, and that was all cool and great, but I am called a creep and a pervert if I tell my cousin her feet look nice after a pedicure. God tells me to respect my father, but when I walk all over him, steal his shit, and call him all kinds of names, he not only doesn't defend himself but freaking thanks me for paying him a visit. I swear to you, if my old man ever ended up in jail, he'd always get smashed. And he'd probably offer the guy a tissue to wipe his dick and then thank him for choosing his ass!"

I thanked Josh for his thoughtful input and then explained that many people turn to religion for comfort and that prayer and meditation can ease grief and give us a sense of purpose and certainty in a world that offers very little of it. I said I am all for it if it helps us become better and kinder people. "A peace of mind is what all of us are after," I said, "and if a prayer can get some of us there, then pray away."

"Jesus is cool and all," Josh replied. "I am just bitching for no reason. But Tupac understood and helped me when I was locked up more than Jesus did. It wasn't Jesus who taught me who to love and hate; Tupac cleared that up for me."

"So, who do you love, and who do you hate?" I wanted to know.

"I love my mother and sisters and the poor," said Josh. "Everyone else can go fuck themselves."

He took a moment to gather his thoughts and then said, "You know what I thought about each night before falling asleep when I was in prison?"

"I have no idea," I said. "What did you think about?"

"I used to imagine watching Tyson knocking out Seldon in person and then riding around Las Vegas with Tupac and Suge. We are bumpin' to LL Cool J and talking about something deep like faith, our moms, conquering the world…some shit like that. And then the fucking Cadillac pulls up, and I dive on top of Tupac as soon as I spot the Glock. I take those rounds in the chest for him with my middle fingers in the air. The cowards panic and drive away while Tupac holds me in his arms, and he doesn't care that I pissed all over the seat and that my blood stained his chains. I am unable to say a word because my mouth is full of blood, and I am about to die, but we make eye contact and nod our heads simultaneously. He tears up a little, holds my head in his hands, and just before my soul frees itself, he whispers, 'What a fucking legend.'"

April Fools

24 March…. I have capitulated. I smashed all the lamps in the house, and now they have to sit in the dark like a bunch of silly bats …. Two weeks ago, I disappeared for three days, and no one noticed. Three days ago, I coughed up enough phlegm to fill a bathtub, but none of them bothered to make me a cup of tea. Yesterday morning, I left a note on the table letting them know I was admitting myself to this forsaken place. I wrote the address and phone number, and the tally is zero visitors and no calls. They don't care about anyone but themselves, and neither should I.

25 March 2020. I slept through the dreamless night. My disease remains. I was a good boy and ate the fake eggs and undercooked bacon they served this morning so that I could take my meds on a full stomach. Got an extra cup of what they call coffee as a reward. The doctor dropped by to see me after breakfast. Three yes-no questions, and he was out. He's a nice enough guy but completely detached. I took offense when he asked me to take a shower. When I returned to my room, the cleaning lady was changing the sheets. She made my bed with enviable skill and fluffed the pillow, which she didn't do for my roommate. She was lovely—pale skin and hair black and curly. She smiled at me as she walked out of the room. I thought about her throughout the day, and it is only now, at midnight, that I am about to fall asleep. The tally of calls and visits from family and friends remains at zero.

26 March. The cleaning lady was in my room again, once early in the morning and again at noon. She undoubtedly makes my bed with more care than my roommate's— she spent ten minutes on mine and a little over seven minutes on his. She speaks passionately in brief sentences of broken English, but I found out where she is from and why she left her country. She's had a hard life, which makes her even more wholesome. So genuine and pure! God bless her. The day's tally is one missed call from my boss and zero visits from "family and friends."

27 March. It's plain and simple: I am in love! The more I see her, the giddier I get. Her hair was in a bun today, and she has the most adorable little ears I have ever seen on a grownup. She gets all bashful and avoids eye contact when she tries to explain the rules about how many pillows and blankets we are allowed to have, and her every movement is dainty

and precious. Goosebumps and hope--it's more than anyone has given me since my high school days in Mrs. Jones' AP history. One call from the bank about suspicious charges—four hundred dollars worth of video game tokens and a lamp from IKEA. I bet they would have called at least once if I had my wallet on me. Other than that, it was not a bad day at all.

28 March. She noticed I shaved and told me I looked much younger. She hummed as she swept the floors: squeaky tone, but no one is perfect. I was so happy to be in her presence that I punched the wall and screamed into my pillow after she left the room. Obviously, she cares about me, and maybe even more than that. I will ask for her number and take her to Old Sacramento for coffee and a stroll. Then, we can go shopping some other day, and she can help me pick some new clothes. The doctor asked me if I wanted to leave since my mood seemed to have stabilized, and I appeared more cheerful and motivated. I stuttered at first and then said that I was, although not as frequently, still thinking about drinking bleach to end my sorrows. We agreed on three more days to think things through and work out a plan. I didn't even ask if anyone had called; It makes no difference. All I can think about is how I can't wait to see her again in the morning.

29 March. A different cleaning lady today… She was pleasant but slow at cleaning and wore too much makeup and jewelry for her age. I held it together until she left the room and was given Ativan by the unit nurse for anxiety. She could have at least told me she had a day off. It's the small things that make you lose trust, and it's the small gestures that keep the relationship strong. Mental torture and fear all day: shortness of breath, cold sweats, and scattered thoughts. I don't think I'll get any sleep tonight.

30 March. No sign of her. I went to the morning group thinking I could distract my brain for a while, but I couldn't focus and remember only bits of what was discussed. Some bearded weirdo talked about life not being a straight line and how curves in the road are to be expected and embraced. "There are lessons to be learned in overcoming obstacles" mantra and "keep on truckin'" boloney. All I want is for her to come back and apologize. Then, I'll be able to embrace my agony and imagine myself as a protagonist of a novel full of ups and downs and stormy adventures. Until then, it's all gloom and doom, and I will not sugarcoat any of it.

I was tempted to call home, but ultimately, I prolonged that battle a bit longer. I don't owe them anything.

31 March. Caught a glimpse of her at the cafeteria during breakfast! I was giddy like a baby, but my ego told me to stay put and ignore her. She didn't even look my way. Not even a glance! She emptied out the trash cans, smiled and waved at a few other patients and colleagues, and then disappeared. She must have found somebody else. Male patients at the hospital are annoyingly and disproportionately more handsome than what you see among the general public, with broad backs and masculine jaws everywhere you look. A professor of economics and a dentist are in the unit next to ours. Our unit has a rugged fellow who draws enviable portraits and gifts them to staff. Lots of wise guys and players as well. I don't stand a chance. I am just angry with myself for being so naive. It's on me, I am the idiot here, but she shouldn't have initiated anything. Leading me on like that wasn't fair, beating up on my pillow like a pinata and tucking in my sheets as if I were some kind of royalty she wanted to impress. She saw me gawking and drooling, and then she pulled away. It's been decided: a jaw implant or a bucket of bleach down my throat are the only two viable choices.

1 April. The doctor came in early to discharge me. He reminded me to take my meds regularly and to keep up the excellent work. The guy is as oblivious as I am. The unit nurse smiled at me and said: "Good luck, and don't return here! You hear me?" She was sweet and made sure I got back all of my possessions. She had charming blue eyes and rosy cheeks with lovely dimples. She pointed to all the lines I had to sign off on and told me to take good care of myself. I was tempted to ask her when she got off work but decided to pull back. Besides, she had a ring on her finger. They ordered a taxi for me, and I got home around noon. Bobby was sitting on the couch playing video games. My credit card was on the table next to him. He asked if I had a fun trip without taking his eyes off the TV.

Anhedonia

"I am here for a different reason than everyone else," I explained to my doctor. "Each of the suicidal patients on this unit knows why they want to die, and I came in here because I can't find a good enough reason to continue living. Unlike them, I want to live. Just need to figure out what for."

After a ten-minute conversation, the doctor was able to pinpoint my illness and diagnose me with anhedonia: the inability to derive pleasure from anything I do or experience. "Tell me something I don't already know," I told the doctor.

I then rambled on about how joy is overrated and how happy folk, mostly, are boring people who are very good at ignoring things. I told him I could tolerate a toothless grandma from some forsaken village who radiates wisdom in her mischievous smile. I also agree that children should be happy most of the time. Kids are creepy in general, but somber kids, with their candor, particularly the perceptive ones who look like they are carrying the weight of the world, are more terrifying to me than thoughts of nuclear war or dementia. For the people in between…I don't know… I am not really sure what I think. I explained that I am more drawn to people who turn on themselves even when they are not at fault. They are usually economical with their words, and their actions leave a negligible emotional footprint. They are too self-critical to burden you with their pain. I probably shouldn't generalize… If there is a reason to laugh, go for it, I guess. I laugh occasionally at Christian rock, presidential elections, bodybuilding, and European baseball. I think what I am trying to say is that I just don't seem to get along with people who make joy and pleasure the end goal of everything.

When the doctor asked what I do for fun, I said that I turn on a basketball game after work from time to time. Still, the sport has become one big joke--the players flop and feign injuries, and half of them are side-gigging as fashion designers and are more concerned with the opulence of their lifestyles than the game they play. I don't blame them, though; I'd probably do the same if I came from nothing and suddenly got my hands on some serious money. I also said I only like music that reminds me of my childhood. Food has become my sole remaining pleasure in life, but I can't cook, and I have gastritis, so I eat oatmeal and apples all day.

I told the doctor that my job is just something I do to stay alive, putting up with crap and pretending to be busy so I don't get fired. I barely make enough for cereal and a roof over my head, but it could be worse. I've been at it for fifteen years, convincing people to buy shit they don't need. It's a soulless endeavor, but I am pretty good at it, and there is not much else I know how to do.

About religion, I explained that I pray twice a day. It's a helpful but time-consuming compulsion instilled in me early on by my uncle, a priest, and I do it even though I don't believe in God. Life would be so much easier if I could trick myself into believing that people get what they deserve. I know that most people aren't genuine believers in anything either, but that doesn't seem to bother them that much. They just carry on with their lives as if they are playing an essential role in a world that makes sense and where everything always works out. I am often jealous of that happy-go-lucky approach to life and would like to experience it, at least for a day or two.

When we got to the topic of my plans for the future, I said that my guess is that no more than ten years of reasonably good health is all I have left, considering all the stress, drinking, and smoking I do. I somehow ended up talking about my siblings and told the doctor that I do care for my younger brother to some extent, but five years ago, I gave him two-thirds of my kidney, and the asshole's gratitude wasn't proportional to the pain I went through. While I still care for the bastard, I don't think I would be willing to risk death for him again. He won't let me see his kids and says I depress them with constant complaining.

I talked a bit about romance as well and explained that I am too preoccupied with myself to be able to offer much to anyone in that department. Besides, I haven't been in love with anyone since childhood. As an adult, I've never met anyone worth impressing.

That was our conversation, and the next day, I asked my doctor to discharge me because a hospital full of idealists without a single doubt in their stubborn heads only lowered my self-esteem. I must be roaming the streets with other lost souls, trying to find something to die for. "I can always return if I don't succeed," I told my doctor. "It's not like I have something better to do."

What I told the doctor was apparently good enough to persuade him that I was no longer dangerous to myself or others. He told me he didn't have a definitive solution for my predicament and that people look for and find their purpose in different places. He then suggested I start my quest by attending a free concert at Cesar Chavez Plaza this upcoming Friday, where the doctor's son's band was scheduled to be the opening act.

"My boy's band is objectively good," said the doctor. "I really mean it. They cover a lot of oldies with their own unique twist. It should be a good time. Maybe you can invite your brother. It'll do you some good to be around people."

"Thanks for the invite," I said. "I'll try to be there, but I can't promise anything. 80's thrash metal is all I really listen to."

The Five T's

"Follow me if you want to know the truths and find out how many of them there are," I heard a hushed, raspy voice say. Looking up, I caught sight of a miniature person dressed in a red gown. It was a male; I could tell by the brow ridge arching over each eye like a canopy. His teeth were shy and hid behind his meaty lips as he talked. On the other hand, his eyes were brash and didn't blink at all. He motioned with a swing of his melon head to follow him as he walked out of the room.

The tiny man led me to the room at the end of the hallway. We tiptoed past Jerome, who was snoozing in his chair and drooling over his chin. The night was crisp and incredibly bright. The moon was out and about, and I had to look down occasionally because the shine bothered my eyes.

The tiny man told me to sit on the bed where two other miniature people practiced different handshakes. The one nearest me wanted to tell me something, but her tongue was tied and unable to produce any intelligible words. The one beside her handed me a notebook and a pink marker and said: "Congratulations! You've been chosen to immortalize the truths. It's a great honor, and I hope you won't chicken out."

"What about all the other tiny people who are more competent and worthy of the task?" I said. "Do they not deserve to immortalize the truths?"

"The past attempts have taught us that some of them might squeal," said the tiny person who handed me the materials. "The leader says that the truths must be guarded by someone bigger until we're the victors of the final event, and only then can they be kiss-fed to the general public. And only to those who are ripe to understand and safeguard them."

The tallest miniature person, who up until then sat isolated on the floor in the corner of the room, climbed and stood up on the table, and he effortlessly turned himself into a granite statue. He stood on one leg and pointed his index finger, along with his gaze, up toward the ceiling. It was not his mouth but his eyes that spoke. They revealed the truths twice as fast as his mouth could because his eyes were two and his mouth one. I, in turn, wrote with both hands at the same time, but keeping up was difficult, mainly because most of the ideas were still foreign to me. I was, however, able to capture and summarize their essence and was overcome with a sense of pride for performing my duty with adequate skill.

Truth number 1.

Tiny people are oppressed by the current regime of big people and their little helpers who come from our ranks. They force us to eat slippery noodles without a fork. They give us a thousand-page book to read without a bookmark. Our task is to get to those who hoard the utensils. When we find them, we'll snatch them and use them how they are meant to be used. With them, we'll teach our people how to properly fork a noodle and get them to stop dog-earing their books.

Truth number 2.

Alone, tiny people would have been torn to shreds by the giant wolves, earthquakes, lightning, and falling trees. Tiny people formed a flat mass during the Great Flood, and together, we floated for weeks until we found land and got off safely one by one. As split individuals, we live sadly and die young. Tiny people need each other like a wet noodle needs a fork.

Truth number 3.

It is the hurt that hurts the most. Holding a grudge can sometimes be a talent. Nourish your anger by taking a minute before each meal to think about those who have wronged you. Fight only those battles where you can leave a lasting mark. Always unleash your anger briskly and forcefully. Blind your enemy with a compliment, and once they let their guard down, submit them and poke their eyes out.

Truth number 4.

Our victory is inevitable because our cause is just. The bigs can learn from us more than we can learn from them. We will undo their teachings and create superior lesson plans. We can and will achieve the final victory alone, but we should try to convince Jerome to join us. The people from the middle ranks are a tossup and can't ever be fully trusted. Those at the top are hopeless.

Truth number 5.

For far too long, we've been robbed of the sweetest fruits—comfortable beds to rest on and acceptance by others as equals. They either ignore us or, from afar, prod and tickle our soft spots for their amusement. Their pity is condescending, and their charity is as good as sin. We want to climb and demand them to slide down until we are above them. Our ultimate aim is a rigid plane to skate on from birth to death.

We propagated the truths around the unit for two days, and we did a decent job, especially considering the conditions we worked under and the widespread ignorance of the tiny people. We managed to convert a solid third. One-third we didn't even approach because they were deeply entrenched in their backward ways and had connections with the enemy. The final third wasn't receptive to the message due to indifference.

On day three, we initiated the revolt, or the "riot," as the enemy called it, and we fought bravely, selflessly, and decisively won the first battles. A brigade of tiny people pounced on one of the night shift guards, tied his feet with bed sheets, stuffed a pair of dirty socks in his mouth, and trapped him in the laundry room. We then got hold of the charts and ripped up thousands of pages of their documented falsehoods and propaganda. We took their reserves of towels, snacks, and gowns and distributed them among the tiny people in our unit, even to those not initially on our side.

The tide turned at around noon. We had made a silly mistake by not disabling the emergency phone in the laundry room before the operation. The captive guard freed himself and called a code, inviting battalions of beefy giants to flood our premises from all sides. Tiny people fought back with all they had--fists, feet, and spit—but were eventually pinned down and sedated within minutes. As expected, a period of tyranny followed.

Congregations of three or more tiny people were disallowed. They still passed out dot-to-dot activity worksheets to occupy our time. Writing implements—even the harmless flexible pens—were now prohibited, and surveillance increased so much that one could no longer urinate without the big dogs counting and recording each of the drops and shakes.

Our holds were extended indefinitely, and tiny people withdrew into their rooms and themselves. Plan B was never developed because our leaders were confident we would triumph. They now hid their faces under their blankets and had nothing comforting to say. All hope was lost.

Most tiny people, to compensate and apologize for their defiance, became increasingly hostile towards the rest who stuck by their principles. I flipped immediately and was as obedient as a guard dog, ignoring my gaping wounds while licking and apologizing for the bigs' boo-boos.

My strategy worked. All it took was to kiss a few rings and polish some boots. They thought they had cured me, and I was out of there ten days after the rebellion. Big Jerome handed me my possessions and escorted me to the front desk. Before returning to the unit, Jerome gave my shoulder a friendly tap and told me to look inside my bag once I got home.

I emptied the bag as soon as I walked out of the hospital, thinking it was chips, a can of soda, or maybe baby carrots, but underneath my clothes and books, there was only a crumpled note that said: "The five T's, brother!"

I looked around to see if anyone was watching me. No people were around, but I spotted a security camera above the entrance doors. I panicked, started sweating all over, and became dizzy with fear. There was no way I was going back there, so I quickly scribbled "Jerome is a traitor. Fire him!" on paper and lifted it towards the camera. I bowed and mouthed, "Glory to the bigs," and slowly walked away out of sight.

Infidelity

My name is Deborah, but people dear to me call me Debs. Today is Monday, month December, date the 20th. I was a teacher for many years until I became gravely ill; I haven't worked and have been vegetating since then. I've been married for thirty years. No kids. Recently, I started dabbling in watercolor, and I've always loved reading. I am in a psychiatric hospital; I believe this is unit D. You guys usually put me on G, but this time, I must have said or done something serious. I am speaking to you, presumably a qualified psychiatrist, and we are here so that you can teach me how to think and modify my self-destructive behaviors.

I will not tell you my last name. I'd rather be tormented than say it aloud. You have to earn my trust for me to give you my last name. You already have it … I can see it on that paper there, but no matter what… I am not saying it aloud. I just don't like to be bossed around like that. I encounter plenty of that at home.

That's up to you to figure out. It wouldn't be authentic if I told you how we can get there. And why do you need to have a good rapport with me? As soon as you have it, you'll no longer respect me. It's not like you'll think about me when you leave; out of sight, out of mind. So, spare me your pleasantries, and let's cut to the chase—what do you want me to do?

I disagree. I can allow myself to generalize from time to time, especially about topics I am well-versed in. When I do it, I do it scientifically—through systematic observation and rigorous analysis. My entire life has been one longitudinal study of male behavior, and the findings corroborate my suspicions about men: You have no standards, and you will stick it in anything that smells a little different. Rich or poor, your core is the same: moss and goo and deceit. Born ugly, you collect nuts and coins for years, then show them off like proud little rodents. Then, at some point in your adolescence, you lose your innocence, turn into sneaky snakes, and impose yourselves on weary women, usually when they are ovulating and find you tolerable.

Talking about him agitates me. He is a lost cause. I gave him multiple chances to partake in maintaining civility in the household. For instance, I'd ask him why he hates it when I go out with him, and he'd tell me that men move faster through space than women. He'd dodge and deflect for a while, argue for the sake of arguing, and whenever things would get too tense for him, he'd just get up and leave. And the first time you storm out in the middle of an argument, the other might just as well pack their things and burn the house down. You are either in it through thick and thin, or you aren't. There is no gray area in commitment.

Of course, I would like that to happen. I would also like to start waking up early, having tea instead of coffee every morning, and making myself a healthy breakfast instead of fried eggs and sausage, but wishful thinking is a fool's errand. I know I haven't been easy to live with either, and I will be the first to admit my flaws, but it takes two to tango. You know what he once said to me? He said he values the idea of living honestly but has a hard time with it in real life because lies get him what he wants more efficiently.

No, I never felt embarrassed. What kind of question is that? Why would I? To feel ashamed, I would have to feel inferior to others. I mean … Do you lose sleep over what you do for a living? The crazy lady honked at me for driving a bit under the speed limit; I snapped, stopped the car, threw my coffee mug at her windshield, and then the cops brought me here. I mean… your ilk blocks thoughts and changes personalities. I threw a bit of coffee on someone's car. Big deal.

The "outbursts" started when a raspberry gummy made me stop caring so intensely and worrying so much about what people think of me. I began consuming gummies "erratically" after Romeo asked to bring her home for dinner. I don't think he'd be alive today if it weren't for the gummies. It's safe to say that the gummies saved both of us.

Well … I told him he could try doing that, but it wouldn't be pleasant for us. He knew I wasn't kidding, so he never dared. You know, for a while, before the gummies, I thought I could go shopping for nicer clothes, make myself prettier, or whatever, but then I looked at him… his skinny legs, the curly hair in his ears, and his shiny little work badge he often forgets to take off well after he comes home. He shows it off as if it's the Medal of Honor. People ask him questions about it, which makes him feel proud.

That's how he met her.

I don't want to discuss gummies anymore. Gummies are good; I can't function without them. Gummies have coerced me into clarity. Gummies help me get to the truth quicker. I mean … since he has his little diversion, I needed to find something just for me. I am too old to plot and delight in revenge. Besides, I am busy with my art and have the book club once a week. He also pays the bills and the mortgage, so there is that… I don't want to be around his ugly mug, but I cannot leave. The plan is to focus on myself and make him feel guilty.

If death weren't a thing, yes, I'd for sure try other drugs. Cocaine sounds like a good time, maybe some hallucinogens, but I would need to do it with someone I trust to give me the appropriate dose. Gummies have helped me express who I am from the heart. It hurts no one. It makes my life bearable and my art more profound. And no one can tell when I am on it; no one knows me well enough to know what I sound like when sober. And even if they did know, why should it matter? I act the same when I am high and when I am not--thoughtful, fun … desirable. Gummies just amplify those qualities.

I can't. I can't because, like I said, I have nowhere to go. He pays for everything. And he never would because my misery is how he likes to be reimbursed. It energizes him. He is impulsive, and it takes him a long time to come around, but he'll get there eventually. We've been through this before. I have to be strategic about how I get my point across--throw a little jab here, cold shoulder there, follow up with a zinger or two when he's trying to nap or watch a game after work. It has to be measured. His ego inflates, and he forgets he's an idiot when another woman's eye is on him. I'll burst that bubble soon enough… Heck, the two of them will do it for me. You just watch. She is an idiot and has no idea who she's dealing with. No one but me is adequately insane to put up with his crap for too long.

Promise you? I won't promise anything I know I won't be able to do. I don't want to lie to you just to get out. What I can do is I can assure you that … that from now on, I won't be wasting good coffee on strangers.

I can also try consuming fewer gummies, maybe one, at most two a day. That's probably the best I can do at the moment. I think that's a good start and a fair compromise.

Angry Meditation

"I am not going to lie to you," my roommate interrupted the yoga session. "I don't see how any of this helps anyone with anything. We are just sitting here and humming like a bunch of confused seagulls. How is cooing in uncomfortable positions going to help us with our problems? Someone please explain that to me."

"It'll help you as much as you allow it to help you," said the young yogi the hospital brings in on the weekends. "I am trying to do my part to the best of my ability, but you must meet me halfway. This exercise is designed to increase mindfulness and help you focus on the moment. The point is to zero in on the vibrations of your vocalization and imagine yourself as a calf pasturing in a luscious meadow, feeling the warmth of the sun rays on your neck, gradually letting go of the past and pushing away the worries you have about what's to come. Only now matters, this moment and none other."

"That makes a little more sense," my roommate interrupted again. "This whole time, I've been trying to channel my inner seagull when I should have been whistling like a giddy California cow from those commercials a few years back. But now I get it; I think you are onto something here. Maybe my life wouldn't be disastrous if I had a dozen tits and could milk myself for morning coffee and cereal."

"Okay… If you don't want to be a calf, maybe you can focus on what makes you tick," said the yogi. "Is there something that brings joy to your life more than anything else? What is something you just can't do without?"

"Shroom burger with a side of seasoned fries from Denny's," my roommate said. "That's what makes me tick. And the ranch dressing they have. I slurp that stuff like a milkshake. Makes my mouth water just thinking about it."

"None of this will be of any use to you if you are this resistant to it," said the yogi. "Meditation obviously won't solve all of your problems, but it could be of some help from time to time if you add it to your routine. Just try to not take it, and yourself, too seriously."

"This guy," my roommate pointed at my head, "won't hum his dog back from the dead. This lady here can bow to Shiva all day long, but Shiva ain't going to house her, get her off the streets, put a hot meal in her belly. And my cancer won't magically disappear if I pretend to be a freaking cow. We've been stretching and chanting for twenty minutes now, and the urge to punch one of you in the face has only gone up. I thought yoga was supposed to be relaxing."

"This is exactly why you need it more than any of these people in the room," said the yogi. "You are a ticking bomb waiting for someone to say something you disagree with to go off. For goodness' sake, it's just exercise. Look how riled up you are."

"I am sorry, but I can't help feeling angry when I am annoyed," my roommate said. "And I don't wake up thinking, 'Man, I can't wait to be angry today.' Shit happens... Someone says something stupid, and I get angry. Why is that so wrong?"

"How about we make a deal," said the young yogi. "What if you just try it today? We only have about fifteen minutes or so left. And if you don't find it useful, you don't have to do it again, and I'll still mark you down as present and give you credit for attending."

My roommate consented and assumed the Cow Pose with the rest of us. He was grumpy for a while, but then his back cracked, and he smiled. Suddenly, he appeared to be all in and transformed himself into a pliant hummingbird in torpor until the end of the class when he became emotional and even shed a tear.

"If I may ask, what's this emotion about?" said the yogi.

"Don't think these tears mean anything," my roommate said. "I am crying because I am one massive vagina, and sweat has been dripping down my crack and stinging my anus. I guess that's karma for you."

"So ... none of this was helpful?" said the yogi. "Not even a tiny bit?"

"No, man," my roommate said. "Honest answer. My pants are all soggy, and I don't have a change of clothes. I'll have to walk around in a gown and watch how I sit so my nut sack doesn't rub against those filthy chairs in the day room. I stayed only because I didn't want to go back to the unit where there was nothing to do. This mindfulness mumbo-jumbo makes zero sense to me. I don't need to be in but out of tune with my thoughts and emotions."

"Thank you for your honesty, I guess," said the yogi, "and thank you for trying. I agree with you. Partially, at least. Yoga isn't for everyone."

"I still get the credit?" my roommate said.

"A promise is a promise," said the yogi.

I Choose Bulgaria

I hit hard my bottom rocks, and it feel very painful and uncomfortable. My body and spirit hurt. I drinked three red wine bottles at party and finished night in field alone with no pants and one shoe. I was lucky my shirt was XXL and covered my kolbas and plumbs. I lay on grass and see flash from the sky and I hear voice from my great-grandfather Bogomil say: "It's time to give up, sinko." And now, after doctor say me I have crazy brain that make fake sound and vision, I must to say I agree with my great-grandfather.

I come to the United States before two years to make money so my family come to nice place, big flat television screen in living room and small flat television in toilet, oval swimming pool, good school for kid; kid then grow up, do some computer fixing or nursing in college, fill our pockets full of big dollar bills so Papa can retire young and enjoy easy life in hot California.

I work as skydive instructor for one year now and make ok money— enough for two small people but too little for two big people with small child. Maybe I try pretend injure my back at work, do big lawsuit, fight corruption with my corruption, but I decide it is too much work, and I am good guy on inside.

Life in America now is very, very concerning, and very, very funny to me. Honestly, it is very funny place, this America. Funny place with funny people. I say to my wife on telephone, "Don't come here, Bisera, stay in Bulgaria and raise Bulgarian big guy from our small Bulgarian boy and not American big guy … because American big guy today is very confusing to everybody and self."

When I grow up as small Bulgarian boy in Bulgaria, my mother said to all people around village they stinky. She say our neighbors you smelly like cow, you stinky like sweaty, you stinky like dusty, but our house always smelly like tart fart. America very much remind me of my mother. It is very much like when American guys say, 'black pot calling black kettle black.'

American guy is very strange man. He worry about wrinkle on

neighbor pants he cannot afford. He have many real problem, but he worry about some fantasy wolf from fantasy land. We have saying in Bulgaria: "Let tiny baby trip on loose socks." It's like very wise saying in Bulgaria… because stupid baby must to learn. America, in my opinion, is very much like my mother and very much like tiny baby in big guy socks— risky business.

American guy is like little baby in big socks, but he also very much like spoiled teenage boy who jacks his penis in bathroom for many hours and shoot sperm on hand towel and sink. His mama very worried and she say him, "Son, we need toilet too." But he never listen her because teenage boy has no respect and only know dick pleasures in life. Mama and papa go to neighbor house to pee and shit because teenage boy is master of toilette all day every day. He come out with sore wrist and shaky knees in afternoon and eat everything in fridge. He complain to mama he tired of cereal and fruit. Boy want only ham and real mayonnaise with olive oil.

You know, American guy is very angry guy too. He is sad but don't know why, so he become very angry. Television say him he is sad because Mexican and Chinese guys will take his job, and wife, and car. But everybody know they will take car only if car is good. American wife is also very sad person, and American job today is shit— no need, they already have, why take?

American television news is better propaganda than Bulgarian television. Bulgarian television say one lie about everything. Very easy peasy for everyone to see what's going on. American television say two lies about everything. After that people fight about which lie is more true and better. But lie plus lie still equals lie, so when television report say big shark family found in ocean, don't go inside water, daddy shark will crush your bones, what I do is I go for little swim in ocean. I never see shark, but one time I see dolphin. Dolphin very nice guy. I enjoy dolphin.

American guy is scared cowboy with nice hat and army gun. He scared some fantasy guys will come and steal protein shake and IKEA lamp from his house. He say they need machine gun to protect self from bad government, but they only shoot clever racoon, cute squirrel, and black neighbor. In Bulgaria we have bird gun at home for when mother-in-law keep pushing buttons on television and in my brain. But it is rule we never shoot her face. I joke, of course. If she deserve, I can accidently shoot her face.

Life is shit, but it is shit with long shape and healthy smell in Bulgaria—no GMO, only organic. Like my grandfather, Spas, say me: "I may not have gold duck in my yard, but I know where I eat, and I for sure know where I play chess." In America I have two regular duck on my balcony, and I eat cold Whopper and chilly cheese hot dog in my car. And nobody play chess in America, only checker. Checker is game for naive people. My pet dog learned checker in one hour, and he decide it is too boring for him. And as far as dogs go, he is pretty dumb dog.

I try America but America never try me. I try to please American guys, and I say him in polite voice, "If American guys don't fight system, my friend, why I must?" When I try to speak my mind, American guys say me: "What you doing here? Go back home, change system in Bavaria." I try to say I from Bulgaria and not Bavaria, and that America is our boss here in U.S., and Bulgaria, and Bavaria. I say to him America is best hide-seek player—it find you everywhere every time, and it make you drink soy Frappuccino and watch Rambo during free time. But I think American guys are right--I need go back where I come from. It sound true in my heart and correct in my brain. In Bulgaria I have my language, I have my family, I can eat delicious zelevi sarmi all week long; I have chess game with friend and organic tomato in my yard. I must to go back to Bulgaria and do my things there because America jerk me hard in circle and spit me out like bubbly gum. American dream make me disappoint and tired.

After I get out from hospital, I will sell my brand-new sectional sofa and coffee table on Craigslist, sit on plane, and come back never. I will miss Taco Bell Cheesy Gordita Crunch and great variety of chewing tobacco, but not so much everything else. The American dream for me is no more. Only two option are in front of me—noose around my thick Balkan neck or Bulgaria, and I choose Bulgaria.

I Don't Care

"Pull up your skirt and get out of the rose bushes!" The group leader started yelling at me and being dramatic for no good reason. People are so freaking jumpy nowadays.

I couldn't get up immediately because a marvelous piece of lengthy poop was already halfway out, and I didn't want it to break off and graze my ankles. It plopped on the ground with one final push and fertilized the flowers. The deed was done. My skirt was up, and it didn't smell. Besides, we were outside, so I don't know what got her panties in a bunch.

"You just ruined outside time for everyone, Darlene," she said. "I will tell your doctor to remove your red band, and you'll lose the privileges."

The privileges are ten minutes in the Rose Garden every other day and going to the stinky cafeteria for meals. I'll live and be okay without those fantastic privileges.

"Fuck you, Darlene," said Amy, my roommate and a supposed friend. "You're one selfish bitch."

I know, and those who know me well do, too, that I am a kind and generous person, so Amy can go fuck herself and take her back-stabbing ways somewhere else. Just yesterday, she praised me when I gave her my chocolate muffin. It's funny how quickly people forget and change sides.

"I told everyone at least three times to use the bathroom before we go out," said the group leader. "I knew this was going to happen. I feel like a fool for even trying."

"I'd also feel like a fool if I was such a Negative Nancy and took everything so seriously," I thought. "The planet is going to hell, the forests are burning, birds are falling out of the sky, the poor are eating the birds raw, and these cowards are frozen stiff after seeing a little ass and pubic hair."

The leader motioned for me to get inside and said, "You broke my trust, Darlene. I am extremely disappointed with you. It'll be a while before you earn it back."

"Boo-hoo," I thought to myself. "Cry me a river, little girl, why don't you? You can take your precious trust and shove it up your ass. Disappointed in me… As if I care. Being left at the altar—now that's a disappointment. It never happened to me, but that would be something to cry about. The way they were acting, you'd think I had kidnapped their kids or something. I'd never do it. I am just saying that that would be a good reason to sulk about. These people have their priorities mixed up."

When we got back to the unit, everyone got snacks but me--they really get creative with their punishments. I didn't care; I had seconds during lunch. They can eat all my food if they want, but I will not let them treat me like a child. I've never begged for anything in my life, and I will not start weeping about a teeny-weeny snack.

I also didn't care when they didn't invite me to the "Sunday Funday" activities in the afternoon. They played Bingo, which I hate, and then they watched 50 First Dates, which I hate even more. The group leader came to get me before the movie started and told me I could join them if I apologized for what I did. I refused and said, "That movie is torture, and so is your presence. Go away and let me rest."

Call me stubborn and childish; I just don't care and don't have time for petty people. No way, Jose, was I gonna give them the satisfaction of humiliating me. I bet I had more fun napping in my room than they did watching that shitty movie, anyway.

Heyoka

I was called in on my day off to assess a patient after he had assaulted my colleague earlier in the morning. I was told that the patient wears his clothes inside out, has poor impulse control, and has several peculiar triggers. He flashed a big smile when I introduced myself and extended his hand to shake mine as I walked up to him.

"I can only give you an elbow," I said. "I haven't shaken anyone's hand since this virus started. My mother-in-law lives with us. She has bronchitis, so I have to be extra careful."

"I have no issues with the virus," he said. "No one ever comes within six feet of me anyway. I guess the rest of you now know what it feels like, which could be good in the long run."

"What provoked the scuffle with your doctor this morning?" I jumped straight to the point.

"Your buddy was a little too complacent for my taste," he said, "and his nose was too round. I punched it to flatten it a little. Things that are green and flat are more pleasing to the eye. That's why we love staring at the trees and fields so much. But you have nothing to worry about. You radiate calm beaver energy, and your nose is alright with me."

"What exactly do you mean when you say that the doctor was too complacent for your taste?" I asked.

"I mean just that," he said. "I can tell that he's had it pretty good in life, and that has always bothered me for some reason. The curve of his belly and the whiteness of his teeth are vulgar. We can't let a proud peacock like that strut through these grounds without plucking some of his beautiful feathers. He's in shock now, but I assure you he'll be happier after the storm. He's led a dull life. He had no stories to tell, and now he has at least one."

"Fair enough," I said. I then asked: "But why do you assume the responsibility to change and challenge people like Doctor Warren? Why take on that burden?"

"I don't enjoy it at all," he said. "I don't want to do it; I get scared every time I try, but nothing would ever get done if I were to wait for others to do their part. People are always trying to get comfortable and hate disturbing those who already are. It takes someone who lives in discomfort to do it."

"Do you ever allow yourself to feel comfortable?" I said.

"Once I rectify all the wrongs, I'll be as comfortable as a lamb resting on a cloud," he said.

"What kind of things do you need to rectify?" I said.

"At the moment, I am on a mission to find out who made fun of Heyoka's weight and sexual performance on social media and make them take it back," he said, and then he became sullen.

"Who is Heyoka, and why would someone make fun of his weight and sexual performance?" I said.

"I don't know, man," he said. "There are a lot of petty people out there who have nothing better to do. I used to go to school with a boy who couldn't do jumping jacks. He'd try his best, he'd bend his knees, and his arms would swing up, but somehow his left foot never left the ground. Before you knew it, he'd spin in circles like a compass and would get in trouble for it because the teacher thought he was horsing around. And guess what? We all made fun of the poor boy. Why? Because kids are little psychos with nothing better to do than pick on the weak."

"I get that," I said. "But I don't yet understand why this Heyoka entity is so important to you?"

"For many reasons," he said. "First, he is innocent, and his feelings were unjustly hurt. Second, everyone needs a purpose in life; defending his honor is mine. Some people have religion, some have families and friends, others have a job or a hobby they like, and I have Heyoka's best interest at heart. Why is that so unusual?"

"I am just afraid that because you devote so much of your time to him, you might forget about you and your needs," I said. "Unless this Heyoka is actually you."

"I am getting tired of this," he said. He frowned and moved his chair a few feet away from me. "I never liked being interrogated, and I am starting to get irritated because suddenly your nose appears rounder, and my hand is involuntarily forming a fist. I am also starting to suspect you have something to do with the scandal. I have a lot to think about, and anger clutters my mind. I'd like you to go away and check in with me tomorrow morning. Knock on the door five times and wait for my response. Don't bother coming in if you don't hear me humming."

"Okay, thank you for letting me know, and thanks for sharing your thoughts with me," I said.

"You are welcome," he said. "Now go away and remember what I said about tomorrow for your own good."

Milan Djurasovic is a Bosnian American writer, artist, and journalist. Milan has published dozens of articles and short stories in various international magazines. His most recent books of fiction include Balkan Grit (2019) and No More Happy Endings (2016), both from Červená Barva Press. His educational background is in psychology and Russian literature. He currently lives and works in Sacramento, California.

www.ingramcontent.com/pod-product-compliance
Lightning Source LLC
Chambersburg PA
CBHW040912010826
48978CB00013BB/1258